Lucy's
Holiday Surprise

Which Lucy adventure is your absolute favorite?

Absolutely Lucy

Lucy on the Loose

Look at Lucy!

Lucy on the Ball

Lucy's Tricks and Treats

Thanks to Lucy

Lucy's Holiday Surprise

Lucy's Holiday Surprise

by Ilene Cooper

illustrated by Royce Fitzgerald

A STEPPING STONE BOOK™

Random House 🏠 New York

For Millie Mamantov. Happy reading!
—I.C.

Text copyright © 2015 by Ilene Cooper
Cover art copyright © 2015 by Mary Ann Lasher
Interior illustrations copyright © 2015 by Royce Fitzgerald

Visit us on the Web!
SteppingStonesBooks.com
randomhousekids.com

Educators and librarians, for a variety of teaching tools, visit us at
RHTeachersLibrarians.com

Library of Congress Cataloging-in-Publication Data
Cooper, Ilene.
Lucy's holiday surprise / by Ilene Cooper ; illustrated by Royce Fitzgerald.
p. cm. — (Absolutely Lucy ; #7)
"A Stepping Stone book."
Summary: With still unnamed twin baby sisters at home, Bobby, owner of a boisterous pet beagle, is worried that his parents will have no time to celebrate Christmas.
ISBN 978-0-385-39130-6 (trade) — ISBN 978-0-385-39131-3 (lib. bdg.) — ISBN 978-0-385-39132-0 (ebook)
[1. Christmas—Fiction. 2. Family life—Fiction. 3. Babies—Fiction. 4. Beagle (Dog breed)—Fiction. 5. Dogs—Fiction.] I. Fitzgerald, Royce, illustrator. II. Title.
PZ7.C7856Lv 2015 [Fic]—dc23 2014026913

Printed in the United States of America
10 9 8 7 6 5 4 3 2 1

Contents

1. Cover Your Ears!   1

2. Vacation!   9

3. Let It Snow   22

4. Games and Names   32

5. Christmas Shopping   48

6. It's Beginning to Look a Lot Like Christmas   59

7. Two Surprises   69

8. The Big Mix-Up   85

9. Lucy to the Rescue   97

Cover Your Ears!

"**W**AAAH!"

Bobby Quinn knew that sound. One of his baby sisters was crying.

"Lucy," Bobby said to his pet beagle, curled up on his lap, "the other one is going to start crying any minute."

Sure enough, the words were just out of his mouth when there came a second *"Waaah!"* The babies were identical twins, and they liked to do things together.

The first seven years of Bobby Quinn's life had been quiet. He was shy. He had spent most of his free time home by himself. Then Bobby got an amazing present on his eighth birthday. Lucy!

Lucy was a little brown-and-white beagle with black spots and eyes like chocolate candy. She was sweet and funny, but she was loud. She liked to howl. She loved to bark. Sometimes she ran around in crazy circles and knocked things over. Life wasn't quiet with Lucy around.

Lucy also liked to make friends. And that helped Bobby make friends. Having friends in the house made it noisier. It was a good kind of noisy!

Now things were noisy in a whole new way. Just a few weeks ago, Bobby's parents had brought his adopted twin sisters home. It seemed as if they hadn't stopped crying since they came in the door.

Bobby heard them in the day and at night when he was trying to sleep. Lucy was the only one in the family who didn't seem to mind the crying. Sometimes she happily howled along with them.

Even sitting there on the couch in the family room, Bobby could easily hear the babies upstairs. "It's loud around here, isn't it, Lucy?" he asked.

Lucy jumped off his lap and onto the floor. Did someone say *loud*? She looked at him and howled. *Hooooowl!*

Bobby sighed. "You're not helping."

Bobby tried to hide it, but he was a little afraid of the babies. The day they came home, his mother had asked if he would like to hold them—one at a time, of course. Bobby shook his head. They were so tiny. He was afraid he might drop them.

Lucy scrambled back into Bobby's lap. He gave her a pat on the head. She looked up at him with her big brown eyes. *Hey,* she seemed to be saying, *are you okay?*

"I just don't know about Red and Greenie," he told her. Right now the babies were called Red and Greenie because his parents hadn't picked out names for them yet. One wore red outfits and the other green so everyone could tell them apart.

Lucy tilted her head.

"I didn't know having babies around would make everything so different," he whispered.

Bobby's dad came downstairs with Red in his arms. Mr. Quinn looked tired. It was the

same sleepy look Bobby was getting used to
seeing on his mother's face.

"The babies cry a lot," Bobby said.

"Oh, I'm sure things will get better,"
Mr. Quinn said. He didn't look sure, Bobby
thought.

Lucy jumped off the couch. She ran over to the chair where Mr. Quinn was now sitting, rocking the baby. Lucy put her paws on the cushion so she could give Red a lick on her hand.

"You know, Dad," Bobby said, "it's almost Christmas."

Mr. Quinn sighed. "I know."

"There's a lot to do," Bobby added. "We've got to get a tree. Go shopping. I want to get presents for you and Mom and Lucy." He probably should be thinking about presents for his sisters, too. *What do you get for two tiny baby girls?* he wondered.

Bobby frowned as he thought about presents. Oh, Santa would bring some, but most of his gifts came from his parents. He wondered if they had bought his presents yet. He was pretty sure they had not.

The baby's cries had finally become little snores.

"Dad . . . ," Bobby began. Then he saw that his father's eyes were closed. Mr. Quinn was snoring, too—and not soft baby snores. More like bulldozer snores!

The house was getting louder every minute.

Lucy came over to Bobby and danced around his legs. Bobby knew what that meant. Bobby got up to take Lucy for a walk.

He looked over at his sister. The baby had a little bit of blond hair and a soft mouth. Had he ever been that small? He couldn't imagine it.

Lucy barked sharply.

"Okay, let's go, Lucy," he said. On the way out, Bobby looked at the corner where the tree was supposed to be. The Quinns always had their tree up by now. Bobby thought about last year's Christmas tree. Full of ornaments. Lots of lights. The corner looked pretty lonely now.

What kind of Christmas is this going to be? Bobby wondered. Would they have time to get a tree? Get their gifts? Would there be any holiday fun at all?

Vacation!

Bobby didn't mind being at school. At least it was quiet. He looked up from his spelling. His friend Candy was standing next to his desk. "When can I come over and see the babies?" she asked. "I thought I would have seen them by now!"

Shawn, Dexter, and Candy were Bobby's best friends in class. Shawn was quiet like Bobby. He liked to draw, too.

Dexter was funny.

Candy, well, she liked to talk. She liked to talk a lot!

"Today is only a half day. The last day before vacation!" Candy reminded Bobby.

Of course, Bobby knew that.

"So I was wondering. When can I come to see the babies?" Candy repeated.

"Well . . . ," Bobby began. He didn't know exactly what to say. He thought his mother might be a little too tired for visitors. Especially chatty visitors like Candy.

"I could come to see them today," Candy said. "Or tomorrow. Or the next day." Candy made a face. "But I really don't want to wait that long. We are going away next week. So the sooner the better! Are they cute?" she asked. "I bet they are cute!"

"I brought a picture," Bobby told her.

"Oh, I want to see it," Candy squealed.

"The picture is for show-and-tell," Bobby said.

"Show me now, and then I can tell everybody how cute they are," Candy said.

Bobby was happy when Mrs. Lee walked into the room. She looked at Candy and pointed to Candy's desk. "Sit, please," she said.

Candy sat.

Mrs. Lee started to tell the class how they needed to clean up before the holiday break.

Bobby wasn't very interested in that topic. He pulled the photo out of his desk. His father had taken it on his phone last night and printed out a copy. It was a picture of Lucy and the babies. Mrs. Quinn was holding the girls, but you could only see her arms. For once, the twins were quiet and peaceful.

"Bobby, do you want to get in the picture?" his father had asked.

Bobby did not.

He wasn't sure why. Maybe it was because the girls were so breakable. Maybe it was because he was afraid he would make them start crying. Or maybe it was because with the twins in his mother's arms, there didn't seem to be any room for him.

Lucy was happy to get in the picture. She had bounded over to the babies. She started licking Greenie's foot. Mr. Quinn took the picture.

"Great!" Bobby's father had said. "They weren't even crying."

As soon as he said that, the girls started crying.

Bobby was so busy thinking about the picture, he didn't hear Mrs. Lee say it was time for show-and-tell. Then he saw Shawn getting up to the front of the class. He was holding a picture he had painted.

"This is our Christmas tree," Shawn told the class. "We got it a couple of days ago. We have ornaments that belonged to my great-grandparents."

Bobby thought Shawn's picture was very good. The tree looked so real, he could almost touch the ornaments. But the painting also reminded him of the empty corner in his house where the Quinn family tree should have been.

Soon it was Bobby's turn to get up in front of the room. Bobby was only a little shy now, but he still didn't like standing up in front of his class. Mr. Quinn had blown up the photo

so it was big. Bobby hoped everyone was looking at the picture and not at him.

"Well, we have new babies at our house," he told the class. He wished he had thought a little bit more about what he wanted to say. "Twin girls," he continued. "They cry almost all the time."

That doesn't sound very nice, he thought. He tried to think of something else to say.

"They are very tiny. They almost look like dolls." Bobby was ready to sit down.

"What are the girls' names?" Mrs. Lee asked Bobby.

"They don't have names yet."

Bobby knew what was coming next. Everyone thought it was odd that the babies didn't have names. His grandparents, aunts and uncles, family friends—they all wanted to know the babies' names.

Bobby explained, "My parents want to wait until they get to know what the babies are like before they give them names."

"Oh," said Mrs. Lee. "Well, I'm sure they will have names soon."

Bobby started toward his desk, but Candy was waving her hand in the air. She had something to say.

"Yes, Candy," Mrs. Lee said, calling on her.

"I think a good name for one of the babies would be Candy," she said. "And then the other one could have a name that rhymes. Like Brandy. Or Sandy. Or Randy—"

Mrs. Lee tried to stop her. "Good ideas, Candy."

But Candy was always hard to stop when she was on a roll. "Mandy. That's another one. Andy, if it was a boy," she continued.

"Of course, it's not a boy. But if it was."

"Yes, well, I'm sure the Quinns will figure it out," Mrs. Lee said.

Bobby hoped it would be soon.

The rest of the morning flew by. The students worked hard to throw out junk, put away books, and get their desks in order so they could start fresh when they came back to school in January.

Mrs. Lee said goodbye to each child as he or she left the room.

"Bobby, have fun with those new babies!" she told him. "Enjoy their first Christmas."

Bobby knew Mrs. Lee was trying to be nice. But having fun with girls who were so young didn't seem possible.

Bobby was surprised to see his mother when he ran outside. He was even more surprised to see that she had Lucy with her.

It was Bobby's job to take Lucy for her walks. That was his parents' rule.

Lucy started pulling at her leash. She was excited to see Bobby!

"Hey, girl!" Bobby ran to see her. Lucy put her paws up on his legs and barked.

Some of the other kids ran over to see the little beagle, too. They knew Lucy. Another time she had run through the town, and no one could catch her. Once she had run all around the soccer field. The coach wasn't happy about that. The team thought it was funny, though, and they had named themselves the Beagles in honor of Lucy.

"Hi, Lucy," Dexter said. He gave her head a rub. Lucy liked head rubs. She licked Dexter's hand.

"Lucy!" Shawn chased the beagle in a little circle. Lucy chased him right back.

Candy picked up Lucy. "Hey, Lucy, I bet you would like a visit from me and Butch over vacation."

Butch was Candy's dog. He was big and goofy.

"I can bring Butch over to meet the

babies," Candy told Mrs. Quinn. "Oh, and I have some good names for them."

The idea of Candy—and Butch—visiting did seem to be a little overwhelming to Mrs. Quinn, just as Bobby thought. But she smiled and said, "I'm sure we'll see you over vacation."

Lucy wiggled out of Candy's arms. She wanted to say hello to some of the other kids.

"Mom, what are you doing here?" Bobby asked.

"Well, the babies are asleep. I thought we would take Lucy for a walk to Main Street," she told him. "We could start to get ready for Christmas."

Finally, Bobby thought.

Just then, Mrs. Quinn's cell phone rang.

"Oh," Mrs. Quinn said. "Right. Okay. We'll come home."

Bobby didn't like the sound of that.

"Bobby," his mother said, "I'm sorry. Dad says Greenie woke up. She has a rash on her arm. He wants me to come home and look at it."

"Okay," Bobby said with a sigh. He took Lucy's leash from his mother's hand. Instead of heading toward the twinkling holiday lights on Main Street, they turned toward home.

This vacation wasn't getting off to a very good start. Not a good start at all.

Let It Snow

The next morning Bobby woke up to snow. Lots of snow. It must have snowed all night and it was still falling.

He tumbled out of bed, and Lucy tumbled out right after him. She was supposed to sleep in the little dog bed next to his, and sometimes she did. Mostly, she slept at his feet.

Bobby made a quick bathroom stop, and

then he ran into the kitchen. Lucy ran in, too. "Did you see the snow?" he asked.

Mrs. Quinn was drinking a cup of coffee. The twins were in their portable crib, curled up next to each other. "I couldn't miss it," Mrs. Quinn said. "Your dad is out shoveling the driveway."

Just then, Mr. Quinn came in through the kitchen door. He stamped his boots and shook snow off his coat. Lucy circled around him. She stuck out her tongue and caught a few flakes.

"Well, it's not too cold out there," Mr. Quinn said. "But it's cold enough for plenty of snow."

"How about some coffee?" Mrs. Quinn asked her husband. "And I'll get some cereal for you, Bobby. You make breakfast for Lucy."

Bobby poured Lucy's kibble into her dish. "Dad, we can still get our tree today, right?" he asked.

Mr. Quinn shrugged. "I'm not sure, Bobby. The roads haven't been plowed yet."

"The Christmas tree lot is out past Pet-O-Rama," Mrs. Quinn added. "They said on the radio the highways were pretty icy. I think the tree will have to wait."

"Wait!" Bobby exclaimed. He could hardly believe what he was hearing. "It's almost Christmas right now!"

"I know, Bobby," his mom said, running her hand through her hair. "We all want to get the tree up, but the roads have to be clear."

"Maybe tomorrow," his father said.

"But . . . ," Bobby began.

Mr. Quinn just shook his head.

Bobby could see there wasn't any point in arguing. He took the bowl of cereal his mother handed to him and jabbed his spoon into it, hard.

The phone rang as Bobby was finishing up his breakfast. His mother answered. She handed the phone to Bobby. "It's Shawn," she told him.

Shawn didn't even bother to say hi. "It's snowing," he said.

"I know," Bobby answered.

"You sound grumpy," Shawn told him.

Yes, I am grumpy, Bobby thought. He didn't feel like talking about all the holiday problems that were worrying him, though. "What's up?" he asked Shawn.

"The snow!" Shawn said. "Let's get out there. We can sled. Or throw snowballs. Or something."

"Okay," Bobby said. Shawn's excitement made him smile. And playing outside did sound better than sitting around moping.

Playing outside sounded better to Mr. and Mrs. Quinn as well.

It wasn't long before Bobby was bundled up. He wore the brown hat his grandmother had knit for him. He found an old pair of gloves. Mrs. Quinn dug up a scarf. Bobby was ready for the snow.

The Quinns' backyard had a fence, and that meant Lucy could play, too. Just as Bobby and Lucy were heading out, Mrs. Quinn stopped them, a bag in her hand. "Here are the snow boots I bought for Lucy," she said. "Bobby, please put them on her."

Bobby made a face. Lucy had worn booties with her pirate costume for Halloween, but they were small and she'd only worn them for an hour or so. These winter boots were bigger and clunky, and she'd be running around in them.

"I don't think Lucy is going to like wearing these," Bobby said. He turned to his father. Mr. Quinn just shrugged.

Lucy had been looking out the window at the snow. She must have heard her name. She jumped off the window seat and danced into the middle of the room.

What's up? she seemed to ask.

"Lucy," Bobby told her. "We've got to put some boots on you."

"Sorry, girl," Mr. Quinn said as he scooped up Lucy in his arms.

She looked at him in surprise.

Lucy wiggled her feet. She squirmed and yipped. Finally the boots were on, and Mr. Quinn put Lucy on the kitchen floor.

Lucy looked at her feet. She didn't move. It was almost as if she had forgotten how to walk.

Just then, one of the babies started crying. Of course, that meant the other baby began to cry, too.

Mrs. Quinn picked up Red. Mr. Quinn picked up Greenie.

"Bobby, will you get two bottles out of

the fridge?" his mother asked. "I think the girls are hungry."

Bobby sighed and went to the refrigerator. He was getting hot with all those clothes on. He took off his hat and gloves and put them in his pocket.

Bobby was handing the bottles to his parents when the doorbell rang. Bobby ran to the door. Shawn was standing there with his younger brother, Ben.

Ben loved to show off his spelling. "H-E-L-L-O!" he said. "It's snowing. S-N-O-W!"

Shawn put his hand over Ben's mouth. "He knows it's snowing, Ben. We're going to play in the snow. That's why we're here."

"Mom, I'm going out," Bobby called. "Where's Lucy?"

He started looking around. Lucy was

nowhere to be seen. "Lucy?" Bobby called. "Lucy, where are you?"

Shawn and Ben stamped their feet and shook off the snow. They came in the house and started looking for Lucy, too.

She wasn't in the living room. She wasn't in the family room. Bobby hurried back to the kitchen. "I can't find her," he told his mother.

"Lucy is in here," Ben called from the hall bathroom. "She's chewing something. It might be a . . . M-O-U-S-E!"

"A mouse!" Mrs. Quinn put her hand over her mouth. "You go look," she told Mr. Quinn.

Mr. Quinn put Greenie in her infant seat. He hurried to the bathroom with Shawn and Bobby right behind him.

Lucy was rolling on the bathroom rug.

She did have something in her mouth. It was black and it was small, but it wasn't a mouse. It was one of her boots, all chewed up.

Bobby looked at his father. His father looked back at Bobby.

"I think you were right, Bobby," Mr. Quinn said. "Lucy doesn't like wearing boots."

Games and Names

Bobby, Shawn, and Ben stepped outside.

The snow had stopped falling, but the ground was covered with the white stuff. There had to be a couple of inches on the ground. Maybe not enough to build a snowman. But more than enough to make a snowball.

Thwak! A snowball hit Bobby right in the shoulder.

"Got you!" Shawn yelled.

Bobby picked up a handful of snow and formed a ball. He threw one at Shawn and got him in the arm.

Ben picked up handfuls of snow. He didn't even bother to make them into balls. He just threw the snow, first at Shawn, then at Bobby.

"Hey, you're supposed to make snow-balls," Shawn sputtered. He had gotten some of Ben's snow in his mouth.

"I don't have to if I don't want to," Ben laughed. He threw some snow at Shawn.

Shawn shook his head. He told Bobby, "You're lucky your sisters are just little babies."

"When's Lucy coming out?" Ben asked.

"Mom's trying to find her Halloween booties," Bobby told Ben.

Just then, Mr. Quinn came out on the back porch with Lucy in his arms, booties on her feet. "Mom says these will be better than nothing," he told Bobby, "but don't let Lucy stay out too long, and don't let her get too cold."

Lucy didn't seem to mind these boots on her feet. Or maybe she was too excited to be outside to care. She looked around, and her brown eyes opened wide.

She had seen a few snowflakes before. She had tasted them on her tongue.

This was something new! This was something exciting! There was so much white stuff to have fun in!

As soon as Mr. Quinn put her down, Lucy danced her way into a pile of snow. Then she ran around in circles, barking happily. Finally she stopped in front of the boys and let out one long howl. *Hoooooowl!*

It was clear. Lucy loved snow!

Ben loved it, too. "Snow just makes me C-R-A-Z-Y!" he shouted.

A snowball fight started—big-time!

Ben made a big, fat snowball and threw it at Bobby. It hit Bobby in the back just as a snowball from Shawn got him in the front.

"Hey, no fair!" Bobby shouted. "That's two against one."

"I'll help you out, Bobby," called a new voice in the yard. It was Candy.

Candy was dressed for the snow. She ran up to the boys with Butch behind her.

Butch wasn't running, though. Butch never ran anywhere. He was slow, and he was lazy. He didn't always smell very good. Today, he was strolling through the yard as if it was the middle of summer.

Butch stopped and sniffed the fir bushes as if they were flowers. He lay down on the ground and rolled around as if he was on a carpet instead of cold snow.

"Come on, Butch," Candy said, pulling hard on his leash. "Get up."

Lucy flew over to Butch. Sometimes she and Butch were pals. Sometimes they weren't. But right now, Lucy wanted someone to play with. Why not Butch?

Lucy looked at Butch still rolling around and jumped right on top of him.

Butch looked up at Lucy with surprise. *Hey, where did you come from?* he seemed to say.

Lucy barked. Butch barked back. In an instant, they were tussling on the ground. The snow was getting stuck to their fur.

"Hey, hey," Candy said, tugging on Butch's leash.

Bobby ran over to the dogs. He tried to pick up Lucy, but she wiggled away from him. Finally he got ahold of her. Butch looked around. He seemed surprised Lucy was gone. All that playing and rolling had tired him out. He headed toward the house and pawed at the door. Butch wanted inside.

Bobby could feel Lucy shivering a little in his arms. "Maybe we should take the dogs in," he said.

Mrs. Quinn sighed when she saw Butch. Last time he had come over, Butch had tried to eat one of her homemade pies. "I'll put them in the laundry room and dry them off," she told Bobby and Candy. "Don't stay out there too long," she added.

Maybe not too long, but Bobby wasn't

ready to come in just yet. There was still fun to be had.

Ben ran over to Bobby. "I want to make a snowman," he said.

"I told him there's not enough snow for that," Shawn said.

Candy looked around. "There's not enough for a big snowman," she agreed. "Maybe we could make something else."

"Like what?" Bobby asked.

"How about a snow dog?" Candy said.

"A snow dog!" Ben yelled. "Yes!"

"Let's make Lucy," Candy said.

"A snow beagle," Ben said, jumping up and down. "B-A-G-E-L."

"That spells *bagel,* not *beagle,*" Shawn laughed.

"Really?" Ben asked. He almost never got a word wrong.

The kids got started. Making a snow dog was hard!

"Maybe we *should* have made a snow bagel," Candy muttered. "It would have been a lot easier."

Finally they got the hang of it.

They rolled a log of snow for Lucy's body. They made four little legs.

Bobby and Candy packed snow and tried to make it the shape of Lucy's head.

"It's too round," Shawn said. He patted the snow till it was the right shape.

It was a little easier to make two snow ears and one long snow tail.

Bobby found small dark stones that were buried in the snow. He used two of them for Lucy's eyes. And one for her nose.

Bobby, Shawn, Candy, and Ben looked at their creation.

"Pretty good!" Candy said.

"Perfect," Shawn said.

"L-U-C-Y!" Ben yelled.

Bobby hoped it would stay cold for a while. He didn't want his snow Lucy to melt.

Now everyone was ready to go inside.

Mr. Quinn was waiting to make them hot chocolate. "All I have to do is heat it up in the microwave," he said with a smile. "And add the marshmallows, of course."

Lucy and Butch were sound asleep in front of the fireplace. Bobby was tired, too.

"Hey, where is your tree?" Ben asked.

"Uh, we don't have it yet," Bobby told him. "And I'm worried we're not going to get one in time for Christmas."

Shawn shook his head. "I guess it's been pretty crazy around here with the babies coming."

Bobby nodded sadly. "I can't even imagine Christmas without a tree."

"Hot chocolate's ready," Mr. Quinn called. The kids scrambled to their chairs.

"Can I see the babies?" Candy asked. "That's why I came over in the first place."

"They're upstairs getting their diapers changed right now," Mr. Quinn told her.

Candy wrinkled her nose. "Wow, babies can really smell. I know Butch can smell sometimes, but he doesn't smell like a dirty diaper." Candy had a thought. "Hey, that would be funny! If Butch wore a diaper? I guess it would be good in the winter. Then I wouldn't have to walk him when it got really cold."

"Yeah," Shawn said. "But you'd have to change his diaper!"

Candy slapped her forehead. "Oh wow, I

hadn't thought of that! Yuck!"

Everyone was laughing when Mrs. Quinn came in with the babies. She sat down at the kitchen table.

Candy jumped up and ran over to them. "Ohhh! They're so little and so cute."

Lucy came running into the room. She put her paws on Mrs. Quinn's lap. Her pink tongue licked at Greenie's foot. Then she gave Red's hand a lick.

"I came up with some names for the babies," Candy told Mrs. Quinn.

"Yes, I heard. Names that rhyme with Candy," Mrs. Quinn said. "Bobby told me all of them," she added quickly.

"Oh, that was just off the top of my head," Candy said. "I have two better names now." She didn't wait for anyone to ask what they were. "They're the names of my two favorite characters in a fairy tale," Candy explained. "It's not a very famous tale like 'Cinderella' or 'Hansel and Gretel' or 'Goldilocks.' . . ."

"Yes, there are lots of fairy tales," Mrs. Quinn said. "Which one is this?"

"It's about two sisters, and a bear comes to their house. But he's really a prince," Candy told her.

"Oh, I remember that one," Mrs. Quinn said.

"It's called 'Snow White and Rose Red,'" Candy said. "It isn't Snow White with the dwarfs. That's a different Snow White. It's kind of weird that there are two Snow Whites. . . ."

"There are two Snow Whites?" asked a surprised Ben. He wiped a chocolate mustache from his mouth.

"Yes, but that's not the important part,"

Candy said. "Let me get to the point."

Bobby and Shawn looked at each other. Candy hardly ever got to the point.

"You could name one of the babies Rose." Candy touched Red's tiny little fingers. "And you could call the other one Snow."

"Rose and Snow," Mrs. Quinn said thoughtfully. "Those are pretty names, Candy."

Mr. Quinn nodded. "Yes, they are. Bobby, what do you think?"

"They're okay," Bobby said quietly.

What he really thought was he didn't want Candy picking out the twins' names. After all, they were *his* sisters. He was sure he could come up with names that were just as good as Snow and Rose.

But at the moment, he couldn't think what those might be.

Christmas Shopping

Mr. and Mrs. Quinn decided not to name the babies Snow and Rose after all.

"They are both lovely," Bobby's mother said later, "but they're not quite right."

Bobby decided to tell his parents what had been on his mind. "I think I should help name the babies," he said.

His mother looked up from fixing dinner. "Why, that's a very good idea, Bobby."

"What do you think the girls should be named?" his father asked.

"Uh, I'm thinking about it," Bobby said.

And when he got into bed that night, he did think about it.

Lucy was snuggled in his arms. "So, do you have any ideas, girl?" he asked her. "What would be good names for the twins?"

Lucy gave a great big yawn. Then she cuddled up a little closer.

"Okay," Bobby laughed. "I really didn't think you would be too much help."

Bobby leaned back on his pillow, and he thought about how Lucy got her name. She was named after his babysitter. That Lucy always made him feel good about himself. So did this Lucy.

"I picked out a really great name for *you*," Bobby said.

By now, Lucy was feeling squirmy. She couldn't stay in one place for too long.

She hopped off the bed and started sniffing around to see what was under it. Bobby was pretty sure she wouldn't find much. Maybe some dust bunnies and some stinky old socks.

What makes a good name? he wondered.

He remembered back before he got Lucy. Other kids scared him. Some of them made fun of him. A few called him Cry Bobby. That hadn't felt very good at all. So Bobby tried to come up with names that were tease-proof.

He considered Jane. No, someone might say Jane the Pain. Jill? No, Jill could be called a pill.

A few more names ran through Bobby's head. He began to realize any name could be made fun of. It wasn't about the name, he finally decided. It was about whether kids chose to be nice or mean. He really didn't understand why some kids wanted to be mean at all.

Lucy jumped back on the bed. The dust she had under her nose made her look as if she had a fluffy little mustache. Bobby laughed as he wiped it off. "Let's go to sleep, Lucy. We've got a big day tomorrow. We've got to get a tree. And some presents!"

But the next morning, the first sound Bobby heard was a sneeze. And then another one. There was no mistaking that noise. His dad's sneezes were as loud as his snores.

Bobby hurried into his parents' bedroom. "Are you okay, Dad?"

His father was still in bed, huddled under the covers. "Well, I god a little code in the node," Mr. Quinn said, pointing to his nose. Just then, Mrs. Quinn came with some tea and a hot-water bag.

"He doesn't have a fever or anything, thank goodness," she said. "He just needs to sleep and rest."

Lucy came bounding into the room. Seeing Mr. Quinn under the covers was irresistible, and she jumped up next to him and tried to lick his face.

"Oh no, you don't, Lucy. Dad isn't feeling well," Bobby said, scooping her up.

Then Bobby realized what those words meant. "If you don't feel well," he said slowly, "does that mean we can't go out and get a tree? Or go shopping?"

Bobby's mother looked at him sadly. "I'm so sorry, Bobby," she said. "I have to take care of the girls while Dad gets his rest."

"Uh, sure," Bobby said as he headed downstairs. His stomach was twisting with all kinds of feelings. He was mad, but he also felt bad about being angry because it wasn't his dad's fault he wasn't feeling well. Bobby was worried, too. Was there going to be absolutely no Christmas at all?

His mother tried to fix things. She called Shawn's to see if Bobby could go over there and play, but his family was heading out to visit relatives. Dexter was already out of town. Even Candy was busy, going to the movies with a friend.

Mrs. Quinn had just hung up the phone with Candy's mother when it rang in her hand. Bobby couldn't tell who she was speaking with. He was very surprised when he heard his mother say, "I'm sure Bobby would be glad to help. I'll send him over."

"That was Mr. Davis, Bobby," his mother said. "He needs some help getting the snow off his front stairs."

"I'm on my way," Bobby said.

Mr. Davis was the Quinns' elderly next-door neighbor. Both Bobby and Lucy liked him a lot. He told good stories, and his house was full of interesting things.

"I sure do appreciate this, Bobby," Mr. Davis said as he opened the door. "Why don't I take Lucy inside with me, while you use that broom on the porch to sweep away the snow. Then we can sprinkle some salt. I don't want to slip when I go down the stairs."

Bobby made quick work of the snow, making sure that everything was clear and clean. By the time he was stomping his feet on the mat, Mr. Davis was opening the door with a cup of hot cider in his hand for

Bobby. Bobby wasn't sure he would like it, but it tasted great.

Bobby looked around as he sat down at the dining room table with his cider. Mr. Davis's house usually just seemed full of things, but today it also looked kind of messy. There were lots of items on the floor and cardboard boxes, too. Lucy was busying herself rolling around on an old red rug.

"So how are those little sisters of yours?" Mr. Davis asked as he brought out a plate of cookies.

"Fine," Bobby said.

Mr. Davis gave him a knowing look. "Makes a difference with little ones in the house, though, doesn't it? It can be kind of rough at first."

That was all Bobby needed to start talking. And talking. Talking felt good. It felt good to tell Mr. Davis all his worries about the holidays and being a big brother. Mr. Davis kept nodding and sipping his cider until Bobby was finished.

"Well, Bobby, it sounds like you are in the middle of a muddle over there. Babies are the sweetest things in the world, but they sure can change plans," Mr. Davis said.

"They sure can," Bobby agreed glumly.

"There are still two days left before Christmas," Mr. Davis said. "Plenty of people do last-minute shopping, and the mall is open late right up until Christmas Eve. I bet you and your parents will get out there. And I'm sure Santa will bring gifts."

Bobby nodded. He knew Santa would come, but he wasn't sure about his parents. Looking around at all the boxes, Bobby asked, "Are you packing up Christmas presents?"

"Oh no. I'm just trying to clear out some of the things in my house. Give them away to charity," Mr. Davis told him.

"Lucy sure likes that rug," Bobby said.

Lucy looked up at the sound of her name. Then she went back to rubbing her head against it and nibbling around the edges.

Mr. Davis laughed. "Must be something about its musty smell. It's been down in the basement." Then Mr. Davis snapped his fingers. "Hey, I've got an idea, Bobby."

"What?" Bobby asked.

"There's so much in this house, and I think some of these things would make pretty good gifts." Mr. Davis waved his hands around. "Why don't you do your Christmas shopping right here?"

It's Beginning to Look a Lot Like Christmas

At first Bobby thought Mr. Davis was joking. Shopping in his house? What did that even mean?

Then Bobby began to look around more closely. Maybe there *were* some things that his family would like as gifts.

"It makes me feel a little bad to have all of these things go to strangers," Mr. Davis said. "It would be great if you could use a few of them as presents for your family."

Bobby started to get excited. "Let's see what we can find."

The next half hour was busy. Bobby sat on the floor, going through Mr. Davis's give-aways. There were a whole bunch of things that he *couldn't* see as presents:

A stack of old pillowcases and sheets.

Two matching green-and-brown lamps with splotches of orange.

Boxes of men's clothes.

But there were also books, lots of books. Books made very good presents.

Bobby picked up one of them. It was a book about the Civil War. It had maps and photographs. It looked practically new.

"My dad would like this," Bobby said, flipping through the pages.

"You know I'm very interested in the Civil War, Bobby. But even if I gave away half of my books on the subject, I would still have plenty," Mr. Davis said. "I think this would make an excellent gift for your father."

This treasure hunt was fun! "Thanks," Bobby said.

"Now what about your mother?" Mr. Davis asked. "How about this?" He reached into a shoe box that had some jewelry tangled up in it. He held out a big, clunky gold bracelet with monkeys painted on it.

Bobby wasn't sure what to say. He didn't know much about jewelry, but that had to be the ugliest bracelet ever!

Mr. Davis burst out laughing. "I'm just fooling around, Bobby. My wife won this at bingo many years ago. She thought it was awful, too."

Now Bobby laughed. He was glad he didn't have to go home with a monkey bracelet.

"Look around some more," Mr. Davis said. So Bobby did. He found a pretty pink glass vase he thought his mother would like. "What do you think about this?" he asked, holding it up.

"Good choice," Mr. Davis said. "Take it for your mom. It will be perfect for flowers."

With gifts for his parents chosen, it was time to look for something for Lucy. "Do you think there's anything here Lucy would like?" Bobby wondered.

Lucy was taking a little snooze on the rug, but she lifted her head at the sound of her name. Then she got to her feet. Many more things were tossed around the floor now. So much more to investigate!

Wagging her tail, Lucy pitter-pattered around the floor. Every item seemed to be interesting to her. She liked the way some of them smelled. Pushing smaller items around was fun. Then Lucy found an old baseball. She picked it up in her mouth and ran over to Bobby. *Can you throw this to me?* she seemed to say.

Bobby took the ball and rolled it across the floor. "This isn't the place for a game of catch, Lucy."

She rolled the ball right back to Bobby. But rolling wasn't nearly as much fun as throwing. She ran back to the red rug and picked it up with her teeth and tossed it around. Now this was fun!

"Why don't you take that rug for Lucy?" Mr. Davis asked. "She seems to love it already."

"She does!" Bobby agreed. "It will be a great present for her."

"The only hard part will be getting it away from her so you can bring it home," Mr. Davis laughed. "There are a couple of grocery bags over there. Take the presents home in them."

Bobby packed up the book and the vase. He had to tug the rug away from Lucy so he could put it in a bag as well. Lucy barked at that.

"You'll be seeing it soon, on Christmas morning," Bobby told her. He went to put on his coat, but Mr. Davis stopped him. "What about the twins, Bobby?" he asked.

The twins? What did babies want for Christmas? Was there anything in this room for them?

Mr. Davis saw the puzzled look on Bobby's

face. He glanced around. "I see what you mean." Then he snapped his fingers. "I've got it."

He pushed a few boxes aside and finally found the one he was looking for. He reached inside and pulled out a large book with big, shiny letters on the cover. It said *Fairy Tales from Around the World.*

"Of course, the girls won't be able to enjoy it for a while—well, *quite* a while, I guess. Someday, though, they will love hearing these stories," Mr. Davis said.

Bobby took the book from Mr. Davis's hands. It was heavy. He turned the pages. There were some familiar stories like "Sleeping Beauty" and "Jack and the Beanstalk," and some stories he had never heard of. There were beautiful pictures for every tale.

"This is great!" Bobby said. He wouldn't mind reading the book himself.

Now it really was time to get home.

"Thank you, Mr. Davis," Bobby said as he and Lucy left the house. "Thanks a lot."

"My pleasure, Bobby," Mr. Davis replied. "And I really appreciate you helping me out."

A few minutes later, Bobby was happily taking off his coat in the warm kitchen.

"You've been gone a long time," Mrs. Quinn said. "And what's in those bags?"

Bobby smiled and shook his head. "It's a secret. A Christmas secret."

His mother looked surprised, but all she said was, "Okay. I guess I can't try to get you to tell me a Christmas secret."

Bobby went upstairs to hide the presents. He imagined how happy his family would be when they opened their gifts. Finally he was sure of one good thing that was going to happen on Christmas morning.

Two Surprises

It was late that afternoon when Mr. Quinn finally came downstairs. He had been sleeping most of the day.

Bobby looked up from the drawing he was making for his grandmother. She was coming to visit the day after Christmas. Nanny Ann always said the only present she wanted from Bobby was one of his pictures. This one was a drawing of Lucy playing in the snow.

He thought his grandmother would love it.

"How are you, Dad?" Bobby asked.

"Much better," Mr. Quinn said. Then he sneezed. "Well, better," he told Bobby.

Mrs. Quinn came in with a cup of hot tea and handed it to Mr. Quinn.

"Not more tea!" Mr. Quinn groaned.

"It's good for you," Mrs. Quinn said. "When you have a cold, you should drink lots of liquids. And I've put honey and lemon in it, so it will taste good."

Mr. Quinn made a face, but he was saved from drinking his tea by the ring of the doorbell. He hurried over to get the door. Shawn and Ben were standing outside.

"Good!" Shawn said. "You're here."

Bobby ran over when he heard Shawn's voice. Before he could say anything, Ben said, "We have a surprise for you. S-U-P-R-I-Z!"

"That's not how you spell it, Ben," Shawn told him.

Ben looked as if he was going to argue, but then his father appeared at the door. And in his arms was a big green tree!

"Hey, can I bring this inside?" Mr. Taylor asked. "It's heavy."

"Why, sure you can," Mr. Quinn said, and he opened the door wide. In came Mr. Taylor, followed by Shawn, Ben, and Mrs. Taylor, who was holding a tree stand.

Bobby couldn't believe his eyes. A tree! Finally they had their Christmas tree!

"Where do you want it?" Mrs. Taylor asked. Bobby's mother led them to the corner in the family room where the Quinn tree always stood. It took a few minutes, but soon the fir tree was in its stand, proudly in its place. It was a tall tree with lots of branches

for hanging ornaments, reaching almost to the ceiling. And it smelled great, too.

"How did you ever come up with such a wonderful idea?" Mrs. Quinn asked.

Mr. Taylor flopped down on the couch. Carrying the tree had tired him out. "Shawn told us how worried Bobby was about not having a tree."

"And we know how busy you've been with the babies," Mrs. Taylor added.

Ben piped up. "We were driving home from our cousins' house and we passed a Christmas tree lot. And Shawn said, 'Why don't we get a tree for Bobby?' So we did."

Bobby turned to his friend. "Wow, Shawn, thanks for thinking of that!"

"Aw, it wasn't a big deal," Shawn said, a little embarrassed.

"Oh yes, it was," Mrs. Quinn said. She

gave him a hug. Then she turned to Shawn's parents. "And it was wonderful of you to get the tree and bring it home for us."

"Yes, thank you," Bobby's father said. Then he sneezed once more. "I have a cold—just a little cold," he added, "but I couldn't get to the tree lot today."

"Well, there's only one thing to do now," Mrs. Quinn said.

"What's that?" Ben asked.

"We have to have a tree-trimming party!" Mrs. Quinn told him.

For the next half hour, everyone had a job to do. Bobby's and Shawn's fathers went down to the basement to get the Christmas tree ornaments. Mrs. Taylor cooed and held the babies while Mrs. Quinn ordered three kinds of pizza for dinner.

Bobby and Shawn had the most fun job.

They made popcorn in the microwave. It was something to snack on while they waited for pizza. Ben was supposed to help them put the popcorn into bowls, but he spent most of the time eating it.

"I'm going to put on some Christmas music. That will get us in the holiday mood," Mrs. Quinn said. "Then we can start decorating the tree."

Bobby had been so busy, he hadn't thought about what Lucy was up to. She must have been taking a nap upstairs until all the hubbub and music finally woke her up.

She dashed down the stairs and into the family room. First she saw all the people. Then she saw the big green tree in the corner. She stopped and stared.

Lucy knew about trees, of course. She

saw them in the yard and in the park. But trees belonged outside. What in the world was a tree doing inside the house?

"Uh-oh," Mrs. Quinn said, looking at Lucy looking at the tree. "We have to figure out a way to keep Lucy away from the tree."

But Lucy didn't want to get near the tree. It was almost as if it frightened her.

"This is Lucy's first Christmas," Bobby said. "She doesn't know about trees, or presents, or, well, anything."

Lucy sat on the couch. She watched while everyone hung the ornaments on the tree and while Mr. Quinn strung the lights. When he turned the lights on and their colors started blinking, Lucy's eyes grew wide.

Then the pizza arrived. Everyone went into the kitchen to eat. There was cheese, sausage, and pepperoni pizza. Bobby liked pepperoni the best. He took two slices.

"This is yummy," Ben said. His mouth was covered with cheese. "Pizza is my best food."

Mr. Quinn laughed as he took another piece of cheese pizza. "Mine too. Pizza is much better than tea for my cold," he told Mrs. Quinn. She laughed along with him.

Bobby was happy to see his family having such a good time.

Finally everyone was full. No one could eat any more pizza. Not even Ben or Mr. Quinn.

"Well, we should be getting home," Mrs. Taylor said as they walked into the family room.

"I guess everything is decorated for Christmas now," Mrs. Quinn said. "All we have to do is hang up the stockings."

Bobby couldn't wait to hang his Christmas stocking. He had had his since he was a baby. It was a little beat-up now, but it was stitched with a jolly Santa Claus. Bells decorated the cuff and made a nice tinkling sound when Bobby pulled out stocking stuffers.

All the stockings had been packed in a small box. Bobby's was on top. But when he went with Shawn to get it, it wasn't there. His mother's stocking and his father's were still in the box. The two new stockings his grandmother had stitched for the girls were still wrapped in tissue paper underneath his parents'. Where was his stocking?

"Oh no!" Bobby said. "Where's Lucy?"

Shawn looked around. "She's in the corner. She's got something in her mouth."

Bobby heard a tinkling noise. He could guess what it was.

He ran over to Lucy. She looked up with a bright red stocking hanging from her mouth.

Bobby moved slowly. He checked out the stocking. It seemed to still be in one piece. At least Lucy was chewing around the heel and not near the cuff. He knew if he went to grab it, Lucy would run, so he held out his hand. "Give it here, Lucy. Give me the stocking."

Lucy ran anyway! She dashed out of the family room and into the living room. Bobby and Shawn were right behind her. They almost had her blocked in the kitchen, but when Shawn turned one way, Lucy dashed the other, out the door and up the stairs, jingling all the way!

Once Lucy got to Mr. and Mrs. Quinn's room, it seemed that she was trapped. Bobby

and Shawn blocked the door. She looked around and jumped on the bed. Then she burrowed under the comforter.

Bobby and Shawn ran over to the bed. They pulled the comforter off her. That

gave Lucy her chance. She hopped off the
bed and flew out the door. She made a dash
for Bobby's room. This game was fun!

The boys were right behind her. "Close
the door," Shawn said.

With the door shut, Lucy had nowhere to go. She stood in the middle of the room, looking around. Nope, no way out this time. She dropped the stocking and stood there panting.

Bobby ran and grabbed the stocking off the floor. He looked it over. It had a few teeth marks where Lucy had carried it, and it was wet around the toe. But no real damage.

"Lucy, bad dog," Bobby said. He couldn't help smiling, though.

Lucy stuck her nose in the air and howled. Game over.

Now it really was time for Shawn and his family to go home.

After lots of goodbyes and more thank-yous, Bobby's parents shut the door. Then they flopped down on the couch.

"What a night," Mr. Quinn said.

Bobby checked on the babies in their portable crib. They were sound asleep. They had even slept through Lucy's mad dash around the house.

Then, to everyone's surprise, the doorbell rang.

"Who could that be?" Mrs. Quinn asked.

"Oh, Shawn probably forgot something," Bobby said. He ran over to open the door.

It wasn't Shawn. It was the second big surprise of the evening.

"Nanny Ann!" Bobby exclaimed. "What are you doing here?"

The Big Mix-Up

Nanny Ann was greeted with shouts of surprise, hugs and kisses, licks from Lucy, and questions about why she had come early.

Nanny held up her hand. "I will tell you the whole story, but first I want to see my new little granddaughters."

Mrs. Quinn put Red and Greenie into their grandmother's arms. Nanny oohed and aahed, cooed and kissed. The babies made squiggly moves. It reminded Bobby of how Lucy wiggled when he was holding her.

Finally she handed the babies back to Mr. and Mrs. Quinn and took off her coat. "Whew!" she said, sitting down on the couch. "It's been a long day."

Lucy snuggled on the couch next to her. It had been a long day for Lucy, too.

"I talked to you early this morning," Mrs. Quinn said. "You didn't say anything about changing your travel plans."

"It was because of our conversation that I decided to come early," Nanny replied. "You sounded so tired, and you said David had a cold. And you were upset that you still had so much to do for Christmas."

"Well, all that's true," Mrs. Quinn admitted. "But how did you get here so quickly? And why didn't you tell us?"

"Luckily, we have three airports in the Washington, D.C., area, so I was able to get a seat," Nanny explained. "And I didn't tell you because you would have told me not to go to the trouble."

Mrs. Quinn nodded. "Yes, I suppose I would have."

"I took a cab here," Nanny continued, "and tomorrow I can stay with Bobby and the girls, and you and David can go out, do some shopping, get a tree—"

"We've got a tree!" Bobby said. He pointed to the family room, where the decorated tree stood in all its glory.

"Oh, I didn't even see it back there!" Nanny exclaimed. "It's beautiful."

The Quinns took turns telling her the story of how it happened.

"Wasn't that nice," she said, smiling. "So

that's one less thing to do tomorrow."

"There's still plenty," Mr. Quinn remarked. "Starting with buying presents."

"Yes!" Bobby pumped his fist in the air. "Presents!"

By the time Bobby came downstairs for breakfast the next morning, Mr. and Mrs. Quinn were already gone.

"All the stores open early," Nanny Ann said, "so your parents decided to beat the crowds."

Bobby wasn't sure his parents could do that. It was Christmas Eve, after all. There would be plenty of last-minute shoppers.

"We have our work cut out for us here, Bobby," Nanny Ann told him.

"We do?" Bobby asked.

"Oh yes," Nanny said. She started ticking

things off on her fingers. "We have to clean the house, start cooking for tomorrow's dinner, wrap our presents . . ."

Bobby looked at Lucy. Lucy looked back at him. That was a lot of things to do in one day.

"And, of course, we have to take care of the babies," Nanny finished.

As if on cue, one of the babies, who were in their portable crib, started whimpering. Nanny picked up Greenie and sat down on a kitchen chair. Lucy ran over and started licking her tiny foot.

"Bobby, when are your parents going to name these adorable girls?" Nanny asked.

"I'm supposed to be working on it," Bobby said glumly.

"What have you come up with?" Nanny asked, rocking Greenie.

"Not too much," Bobby confessed. "Do you think the names should rhyme, like my cousins, Brian and Ryan?"

"Maybe one set of rhyming names in the family is enough," Nanny said.

"Then I tried to think of my favorite names. But my favorite girl's name is already taken," Bobby said. "Lucy, of course."

Lucy gave a little bark at that.

"We will work on it today," Nanny said. "We'll come up with something."

Bobby walked over to his grandmother and Greenie. He patted the baby on her head. "I promise we won't let you go without a name much longer."

He hoped that was a promise he could keep.

The next couple of hours flew by. Nanny Ann had told him that his parents were bringing home the turkey for tomorrow's dinner, so she made a green bean casserole and then started baking Christmas cookies. Bobby helped with that. Well, he helped by eating a couple of them when they came out of the oven.

"Only one more, Bobby," Nanny said. "We want to have a few left for tomorrow."

Lucy would have liked a cookie, too, but Bobby knew cookies weren't good for dogs. He gave her one of her chewy bones. She looked up at him with a sad expression, but she took it anyway and started gnawing away.

Then it was time to wrap the presents.

"I'm not very good at wrapping," Bobby confessed.

"I am," Nanny told him. "And I brought a couple of holiday bags for things that might be too hard to wrap."

Bobby was pleased about that. He could just put some tissue paper around the picture he had drawn for his grandmother and place it in a bag.

He brought out his presents for his parents and the babies. Nanny Ann was impressed. "Where did you get all these?" she asked.

Bobby told her about his morning at Mr. Davis's house.

"Wasn't that sweet of him," Nanny exclaimed. "I'm sure your parents are going to love their gifts. And someday, the girls will love this beautiful book."

They were interrupted by a knock at the door. Nanny went to answer it with Bobby and Lucy right behind her.

It was Mr. Davis. Bobby's grandmother had met Mr. Davis at Thanksgiving. "Thank you for giving Bobby all those wonderful things for gifts," she said.

"My pleasure," Mr. Davis responded.

"Would you like to come in?" Nanny asked.

"Oh no. My daughter is waiting for me in the car. I'm going to her house for Christmas. I just wanted to bring these over." Mr. Davis was holding a bouquet of flowers. He gave them to Nanny. "Have a nice holiday."

"Why, thank you!" Nanny replied. "You too."

She closed the door and looked at the flowers. "Aren't these pretty," she said. "White mums and lots of red holly."

"They are nice," Bobby said. The red holly gave the bouquet a festive look.

Nanny brought the flowers into the kitchen and put them in a vase. Then the babies started crying. Nanny went over and picked up one and then the other. "Oh, I think they need their diapers changed."

Diaper changing was often a smelly event. Bobby was happy when his grandmother didn't ask him to help.

He was tossing around a ball with Lucy when he heard his grandmother call from upstairs. "Bobby, come up here. I need you."

Bobby didn't like the worried sound of her voice. He rushed up the stairs with Lucy right behind him. "What's wrong, Nanny?"

The babies were on their changing table. They were wearing their diapers, but nothing else. "Uh-oh," Bobby said.

He knew right away what was wrong. His parents always changed one baby first and put her back in the correct-color onesie. Then they would change the other baby and

put her in the other color. The girls looked so much alike, it was impossible to keep them straight unless one was kept in red and the other in green. Now the outfits they had been wearing were in the hamper. Nanny hadn't gotten new ones out of the drawer.

"I don't remember which girl was in which color," Nanny groaned. "Oh, Bobby, I've mixed up the babies!"

Lucy to the Rescue

Bobby was shocked! Mixed-up babies! He hoped his parents wouldn't come home for a while. Maybe he and Nanny could solve this problem before they arrived. But how that would happen, he didn't know.

"What are we going to do?" Nanny asked with alarm. "Can you tell them apart?"

Bobby looked at the girls. They both had a few strands of blond hair on their heads. They both had big blue eyes, the same tiny button noses, and little rosebud lips.

"Your mother told me how careful she has to be to make sure each girl is in the right color because they are identical. Oh dear, oh dear," Nanny Ann moaned.

Bobby tried to think of something to make his grandmother feel better. "Maybe it doesn't matter," he said. "They don't even have names yet. We can just start over."

Nanny shook her head. "That doesn't seem right. One is Red and one is Greenie. Your parents have been calling them that for days," she explained. "I can't just switch them."

Bobby and his grandmother stared at the girls. What should they do?

Then one of the babies started crying. Nanny Ann picked her up. She sat down in the rocking chair with the baby. Nanny looked as if she was going to start crying, too.

Lucy stared at Nanny and the baby. She seemed to understand that everyone was upset. She trotted over to the rocking chair. She put her paws on the seat. She started licking the baby's foot.

"Wait a minute!" Bobby exclaimed. "That baby is Greenie!"

Nanny gave Bobby a startled look. "How do you know?"

"Lucy always licks Greenie's foot. And she licks Red's hand," he told her excitedly.

"Are you sure?" Nanny wanted to know.

"Yes. I never really thought much about it, but I see her do it all the time," Bobby said.

The baby stopped crying as Lucy licked her foot. Nanny used her free hand to pat Lucy's head. "Lucy, you are the best dog in the world! You've saved the day!"

"Absolutely," Bobby said. "Thank you, Lucy."

Lucy stepped away from the chair and nodded her head. It was almost as if she was taking a little bow.

By the time his parents arrived home, everything was back to normal. Each baby was dressed in the right outfit. The table was set, ready for Christmas dinner, with Mr. Davis's flowers in a vase. The house was neat and smelled like cookies.

"How did everything go?" Mrs. Quinn asked when she came into the house, her arms full of packages.

"Oh, fine," Nanny Ann said.

Nanny had already told Bobby they would wait until after Christmas to tell Mr. and Mrs. Quinn about the mix-up. "Let's just enjoy the holiday."

Bobby agreed.

After the Quinns had taken off their coats and put away the packages to wrap later, they sat down on the couch. Nanny had coffee and cookies ready for them. She turned on the radio to the station that played holiday songs and Christmas carols.

Mr. Quinn took a sip of coffee. "Thanks, Ann. This is all perfect. And I love listening to Christmas carols. I think that's my favorite thing about the holidays."

Mrs. Quinn looked around. "The house looks so nice, Mom. Where did the flowers on the dining room table come from?"

"Mr. Davis brought them over," Nanny told her.

"How sweet. I love the way the holly looks in the bouquet. You only see holly berries around Christmastime. I wish you could get them all year long, they are so bright and cheerful," Mrs. Quinn said.

Bobby was on the floor, petting Lucy. Suddenly he had an idea. Was it a good idea? He thought it was a great idea! He hoped his own parents would feel the same way.

Bobby took a deep breath. "Mom. Dad. I think I know what we should name the babies," he said.

All the adults turned in his direction.

Bobby cleared his throat nervously. "Okay. Well, Dad, you said you love carols, and, Mom, you love holly. Those are both girls' names, right? Carol and Holly? And if that's what we name the twins, it would be like we'd have a little bit of the holidays with us all year long."

For a moment there was silence. His parents looked at each other. Bobby was afraid no one liked his idea.

Then his father clapped his hands, and his mother looked as if she was going to laugh and cry at the same time. His grandmother beamed at him.

"Perfect!" Mrs. Quinn said. "Just perfect."

"Our Red can be Holly, 'cause holly is red," Mr. Quinn said. "And Greenie will be Carol."

Bobby and his grandmother exchanged looks. Finally the babies had names. Bobby gave Lucy a hug.

"Hey, why don't we take a picture together, so we'll remember the moment the babies got named," Bobby's father said.

He got out his phone and arranged everyone to get together. Nanny Ann was holding Holly, Mrs. Quinn held Carol, Bobby and Lucy kneeled in front, and Mr. Quinn crowded next to them holding the phone.

"Smile, everyone," he said.

Bobby's smile was wide. After all, he was spending Christmas with his parents, his grandmother, the new sisters he had named, and the best dog in the world.

"This is going to be absolutely the greatest Christmas ever, Lucy!" Bobby said, giving Lucy a hug.

Lucy barked. She absolutely agreed!